mclearmusic@mac.com

To Hailie

FAIRY TALE
CHRISTMAS

Michael McLean

Michael McLean
AND
Scott McLean

ILLUSTRATED BY JASON QUINN

SHADOW
MOUNTAIN

FOR BUCKY AND SADIE

Just past the breath
Where it seems like it ends
Is precisely the place
Where a new one begins

Art direction by Richard Erickson
Design by Sheryl Dickert Smith

Text © 2014 Michael McLean and Scott McLean
Illustrations © 2014 Jason Quinn
Song lyrics © 2014 Shining Star Music (ASCAP)

Visit us at ShadowMountain.com

Library of Congress Cataloging-in-Publication Data
McLean, Michael, 1952– author.
  Fairy tale Christmas / Michael McLean and Scott McLean.
    pages cm
  Summary: When the Fairy Tale Villains kidnap Santa Claus, the Fairy Tale Heroes must decide if they will sacrifice their happiness so that Santa can bring Christmas to all the children of the world.
  ISBN 978-1-60907-930-7 (hardbound : alk. paper)
1. Santa Claus—Juvenile fiction. [1. Santa Claus—Fiction. 2. Fairy tales—Fiction. 3. Characters in literature—Fiction. 4. Humorous stories.]
I. McLean, Scott (M. Scott) author. II. Title.
  PZ7.M4786995Fai 2014
  [Fic]—dc23   2014019047

Printed in the United States of America
Publishers Printing

10   9   8   7   6   5   4   3   2   1

Contents

1. The Abominable Stew   1

2. Ever after the End   19

3. So Much Good in the World   32

4. A Singing Telegram for Santa   43

5. It's a Dream Sleigh   59

6. Surprise Parties   66

7. We Can't Go Back   100

8. On One Condition   109

CONTENTS

9. Logistical Nightmare or Dream
   Come True?   118

10. The View from Up Here   125

11. The Spirit of Christmas Is ... Magical!   131

    The End ... ?   139

    Epilogue   146

    Important Note   152

CHAPTER 1

The Abominable Stew

ONCE UPON A CHRISTMASTIME, just a few bedtime stories before Christmas Eve, and long after every "happily ever after" ending, a clandestine meeting was being held. Of course, you'd expect such a meeting to be undercover, underhanded, sneaky, and dishonorable, but that's not why it was called a clandestine meeting. Before this meeting, at the annual Long Ago Island Job

Fair for disenchanted fairy-tale villains seeking new employment, a bossy stepmother, a hungry Giant, a vengeful six-foot Fairy Queen, a self-absorbed Drama Queen, and a creepy little schemer with a truly bizarre name decided to skip the job fair altogether and call themselves "The Clandestines." They did this *partly* because all of them were, in fact, underhanded, sneaky, and dishonorable, but it was *mostly* because "The Clandestines" made for a much better sounding name than "Evil Fairy Tale Villains." And "The Temptations" had already been taken.

On this, their first official gathering of the winter solstice, they all arrived at the Abominable Snowman Café, a sketchy little dive carved out of a barren copper mine on the outskirts of the North Pole. Owned and operated by a grumpy old prospector named Barnaby "Tundra" T. White and infamous for a rancid herbal tonic he brewed himself called "Tundra T's Thistleweed Tea." Barnaby was so convinced it contained healthy properties that he insisted on adding it to every recipe— even though it made everything taste disgusting. So the café was a terribly unpopular place to visit, but that only made it the perfect place for the Clandestines to meet. No one with any inclination to do anything good had ever visited the café. And that's why it was one of the few places left in the world where fairy-tale villains like the Clandestines could still disappear.

One by one they burst through the doors of the café wearing their matching black leather jackets with "The Clandestines" etched in bold lettering across the front. Medoza, the vengeful Fairy

Queen, who had designed the jackets herself, took pride in how intimidating they all looked together. She had also made a special set of clothes for their creepy little schemer, who was spying on Santa's workshop and gathering intelligence for a very clandestine operation.

Rumpelstiltskin, however, did not feel intimidating when he walked into the café wearing *his* jacket: a traditional elves' workshop gold-button blazer with puffy white collar and cuffs. His red velvet pants ended at his knees, where a pair of red-and-green stockings disappeared into little brown slippers that curled at the toe. And if that wasn't bad enough, hanging from the tips of his slippers were two tiny bells that jingled happily with every step. It was enough to drive anyone mad.

"Hey, Rump. What's the word?" Snow White's dangerously vain Drama Queen asked.

"Don't call me that," the little man snapped as he adjusted the fur cap on his head. "I hate it when you call me that."

"I thought you hated being called Stiltskin," Cinderella's wicked stepmother, Agatha, said.

"I hate that, too. Just call me Goldman." Twisting around in his chair, he called for a waiter. "Hey! Is anyone going to take our order, or do we have to cook it ourselves?"

From a nearby table, old Barnaby White (who, in addition to being a terrible cook, was also the only waiter in the place, which only contributed to the café's abysmally slow and short-tempered service) spitefully walked over to take their order.

"This better not be on separate checks," Barnaby growled.

"It's not," said Medoza. "Give it to him." She pointed at Goldman.

"What? Wait! Why me?"

"Because you're the one who can turn straw into gold," she snapped. "It's not like any of us are working right now." The others nodded in agreement.

"Fine," Goldman growled. "How's the stew?"

"Abominable," said Barnaby matter-of-factly.

"Just how we like it," the Drama Queen said gleefully as all the Clandestines cackled in unison. Well, everyone cackled except the dim-witted Giant, who had the smallest brain in the room but somehow possessed a much more discerning palate than everyone else.

"Do you have any Fee-Fi-Fo-Fum sauce?" the Giant asked. Perched on two stools—one for each half of his ginormous backside—he barely fit beneath the café's ceiling.

"Red or green?" Barnaby asked.

"Red, like the blood of an Englishman." The Giant laughed at himself.

"Yeah, like I haven't heard that one before," Barnaby said rudely. He belched, scratched his beard and his backside, and sluggishly made his way back to the kitchen to fetch their stew and a bottle of red Fee-Fi-Fo-Fum sauce. In the meantime, the Clandestines got down to the real business of their meeting: plotting revenge.

For years, they had all been searching for a way to change the endings of their stories. They were tired of good always triumphing over evil. They were sick to death of love conquering all. They'd had it up to their eyeballs with happy endings. Things needed to change, and they were bound and determined to make it happen at any cost.

The problem was, only heroes were awarded the endings of the stories. And once the stories were told, only the heroes could change the endings, or "give them away." And they had to be *given*; they could never be taken. Somehow the Clandestines had to entice the fairy-tale heroes to willingly give up the endings of their stories, a feat believed to be impossible. That is, until now.

"So what do you have for us, Goldie?" Agatha asked.

"Goldman. It's Goldman. Not Goldie." He gritted his teeth so hard it was a wonder they didn't crack.

"Okay, okay. *Goldman*," Agatha said. "Just talk already. The suspense is killing us."

The little man picked up his rotten-thistle-weed-eggnog shot and gulped it down. The noxious drink made his eyes water and he sighed with pleasure. "Well, something big is going down *this* Christmas Eve."

"I know what it is! I know what it is!" the Giant interrupted. "Santa's delivering presents, right?"

Everyone at the table rolled their eyes. "Yes, of course, you big, dumb giant. Santa's delivering presents," Goldman snapped. "But this is different. The elves have been working overtime since Mother's Day, building more toys than anyone has ever seen! They've been working so much that representatives of the North Pole Elf and Reindeer Labor Association—the NPERLA—are demanding that Santa rewrite their contracts to include overtime pay with extra hugs, kisses, and tickles—"

The Giant made a retching sound.

"I know, I gagged too. But there's more. They also want twice as many candy canes and cookies upon completion and—get this—a brief forum to express their grievances!" The group was silent for a moment, failing to see the significance of this news.

"So what?" Medoza asked, unimpressed.

"What do you mean, 'So what?'" Goldman exclaimed. "This is historic! Santa's elves are the hardest working, non-complaining creatures in existence, and they've actually been so overworked they need to unionize!"

"But what does that mean?" the Giant asked,

not really understanding what had been said, only that there seemed to be a whole lot of kissing going on at the North Pole.

"It means I found a way to get what we want! Trust me, if I can do anything, I can anticipate how a person might become desperate for help, and I know how to take advantage of that. I happen to know a thing or two about magic, and what it takes to make impossible things happen in one night. I've also done the math. Santa's sleigh is one hundred and fifty years old. It's never delivered so many toys before." Goldman leaned forward and spoke in a whisper. "Santa doesn't even know this yet, but the Big Guy is gonna have to double back to the North Pole more than once to get all those toys delivered. His schedule has never been this tight. And for the first time in history, he's not going to be able to deliver them all in time."

"Well, don't we feel bad for him," the Drama Queen added sarcastically.

"No. Don't you understand?" Goldman hissed. "This is perfect. The closer he gets to Christmas, the more desperate he's gonna be for solutions to this problem. The elves might be great builders, but they're useless when it comes to delivering presents. He's going to need all the full-sized help he can get!"

"So how do *we* get Santa Claus?" Agatha interjected.

"You asked me to find a way to get Santa out of his workshop *before* his travel security charms activate on Christmas Eve. Well, this is it! Failure to deliver all the presents is not an option for Santa

Claus. If we can lure him out of the workshop with the promise of a bigger, more powerful sleigh, I'm telling you, he'll jump at the chance without asking too many questions!" Goldman chuckled. "That, my friends, is his Achilles' heel!"

"I don't get it." The Giant looked at them with a puzzled expression. "Does he need a new sleigh or new shoes?"

Goldman couldn't believe his ears. "Really? Somebody get this genius back to his beanstalk. Look, you want to get Santa, the key is a new sleigh. We just need to avoid any suspicion he might have about it. Make it look like it's being offered by anyone remotely trustworthy . . . and HE'S OURS!"

Agatha's thin lips twisted into a frown. "And how do we do that?"

"That's your problem. I usually try to convince the mark that I'm their trustworthy source, but I'm just an inside man on this project. You're the ones that need to tempt him out of the workshop." Goldman leaned back in his chair. "I sure hope this assignment doesn't turn out to be a big waste of time. I mean, look what happened with the Easter Bunny."

"Of course you'd bring that up again. How many times do I have to tell you we simply misjudged the situation?" Agatha glared at him.

"Look, I could've told you before I even left that the Easter Bunny couldn't give us the kind of leverage Santa Claus can. But you wouldn't listen." Goldman folded his arms over his chest.

"We were exploring our options and it just didn't work out," Agatha growled. "It happens."

"Knock it off, you two," the Drama Queen said, but by that time Goldman and Agatha were really going at it. Their angry voices grew louder with each sentence until a few stern looks from those at the tables around them shamed them into silence.

For a moment, no one at the table spoke. They all sat staring at the sickly, dull green flame from the table candle Barnaby made from the earwax of bridge trolls and forest goblins.

"Well, what do you want from me?" Agatha asked Goldman angrily. "An apology?"

Goldman lifted his chin and glared at her. "That would be nice."

As if on cue, all three women, in an almost musical unison, said, "We don't do *nice*!"

Goldman felt his lips tremble. An annoying

tickle started low in his belly. He tried to fight it off. He thought every angry thought he could, but he couldn't stop the burst of laughter that erupted from his mouth. After a short pause, they were all laughing, including the Giant, who wasn't really sure what they were laughing at, but he joined in all the same.

Between gulps of laughter, Goldman managed to get out, "It would be pretty strange if a club calling itself the Clandestines did *nice,* eh?"

The group laughed a bit more; then the stew arrived and they all dug in.

Halfway through dinner, Goldman pushed his chair back and stood up. "It's getting late. If I don't get back soon, the elves may get suspicious. Send me a note or something. Let me know what we're going to do from here. And do it quick," he grumbled. "I can't take much more of this." Much to his irritation, his boots jingled happily as he wove his way past every tough-looking costumer of ill repute at the Abominable Snowman Café.

On his way out the door, he heard Barnaby call out, "Hey, Twinklebells, you wanna pay this check before you go?"

Unwilling to take a single embarrassing jingle step that wasn't absolutely necessary, Goldman called back to the counter, "Just put it on my tab, Barn!" Then, glaring at a particularly rough look-ing character, he said, "I ain't no Twinklebells. I downed every drop of that abominable stew!" He hiked up his red velvet knickers and proudly jingled out the door.

CHAPTER 2

Ever after the End

THE ENCHANTED PROMISE that gives a fairy-tale hero a fairy-tale ending is unbreakable! The pageantry of the event is really quite something. It happens in places beyond storybook pages, right after the last word is read. The child who reads it takes in a deep breath and exhales the happiest thoughts. That breath is carried by lights and by winds that swirl on currents from clouds to the stars. Then zoom, like a comet, it crackles and flares, then shoots out of sight to a land far away, where the fairy-tale heroes all live.

When it finally arrives, it bursts like a rocket in a fireworks show. But before all of the little glowing embers fall softly to the ground, they float back together and form delicate spheres of breathtaking light that land peacefully in the palm of every hero's hand.

And just as the child is starting to dream about faraway places, the fairy-tale hero holds those little spheres of light close to his or her heart. And as the light flows through his or her soul, the child's happiness in that moment becomes as much a part of the hero as their fairy-tale ending, forever their own, theirs to change, to keep, or to give as they choose.

The Clandestines, of course, knew all about this hullabaloo, and it made them want to barf.

With Goldman's departure, the motley crew of fairy-tale villains was anxious to process the information they'd received from their undercover spy. They had almost given up on the idea of kidnapping Santa Claus.

It was far too ambitious. He was far too protected. He was held in the highest esteem. Children everywhere loved him, and they often defined the most memorable moments of their lives by what he brought them at Christmastime. All of that love and adoration made his workshop a fortress impenetrable to every evil spell in their arsenal. No one could touch him up there! *If* Santa Claus could be lured away from the North Pole prior to Christmas, they might have a chance. They knew the fairy-tale heroes would do anything to preserve joy and holiday happiness for the children of the world. That's why kidnapping Santa Claus was the only way for the Clandestines to get what *they* wanted for Christmas.

• • •

Before long, Barnaby announced it was closing time. When he approached their table to take away their empty dishes, they waved him off.

"It's closing time," said Barnaby with an irritated twist of his lips.

"Is it?" Agatha asked.

"Yes, it is!"

"Don't let the door hit you on the way out, then," she said as she turned back to the group.

"I don't think you understand. You're the ones

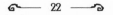

who need to leave," Barnaby growled. "Now. I'm locking up."

"I don't think so," the Drama Queen answered. "We need to borrow the place for a bit of scoundreling. Leave the keys. We'll lock up when we leave."

Barnaby was fuming. "But you . . . this . . . " he sputtered. "I'll be charging Goldman's tab a ridiculously high fum-fo-fi-fee!"

"That's fine," said the Giant. "He's loaded."

"Ugh. Very well. But I'm getting sick of this. You do this all the *time*," Barnaby complained and then asked, "You know where to leave the keys?"

"Under the phony pile of dog poop in the yard, right?" the Giant called back.

"You got it." Barnaby blew out a few candles and headed for the door. "Oh, and be careful when hiding the key. The Big Bad Wolf came by here earlier on his way to visit the three pigs. Let's just say he fertilized the lawn."

The ladies groaned and wrinkled their noses. The Giant just laughed.

Agatha sat up and asserted herself as the leader of the meeting. "All right, settle down. I think we have the information we've been waiting for. So the proposal for kidnapping Santa Claus and holding him for ransom is *still* a go." All the Clandestines cheered with sinister glee. "Now, as Goldman suggested, we need to make it look like a brilliant new sleigh is being given to Santa from someone he trusts. I think it's obvious who that person should be. It's Cinderella!"

"Why her?" the Drama Queen demanded. "Why not Snow White?"

"Oh, please!" cried Medoza. "Beauty is the only one who would think to give such a gift!"

"Jack might do something like that," the Giant suggested.

"What do you know, Giant?" the Drama Queen jabbed. "Nothing, that's what! Now keep your mouth shut."

"Hey," said the Giant. "Don't be like that."

The argument almost came to a boil before Agatha rose above it. "All right, all right, all right! New suggestion! We'll convince Santa that his sleigh is a group gift from *all* of the fairy-tale heroes."

"All of them?" asked the others.

"That's right. It'll be such an attractive, extravagant new sleigh that it will be even more believable as a gift from all of them." Agatha moved to the café's chalkboard and erased the specials of the day to start making notes.

"But doesn't that give Santa more of a chance to find out the sleigh is bogus if he has more people to call and ask about it?" asked Medoza.

"Fair question." Agatha agreed. "That's why we're not going to give him a chance to call anyone. It'll be so close to Christmas Eve, and we'll get him so excited about the new sleigh, he'll rush off to get it without a second thought. The timing has to be perfect.

"But I'll need your powers of disguise, Drama Queen. Are you up for it?"

The Drama Queen smiled. "Well, my range of disguise isn't what it used to be, Agatha, but you tell me what you have in mind, and I'll see what I can figure out. Don't do anything with a big nose, or huge wart, or sea-hag skin. Give me something that requires a theatrical stretch."

Agatha considered for a moment or two, and then she asked, "Have you ever done a singing telegram?"

The Drama Queen's perfectly sculpted eyebrows lifted. "A musical? I *love* it!"

Agatha went back to her chalkboard of evil ideas and mapped out the finer points of her plan. "I think this really could work," she mumbled to herself.

"Oh, I agree!" Medoza said as she looked at the chalkboard.

"It's the perfect direction," confirmed the Drama Queen.

"Oh yeah, now I see what—" the Giant said, pretending; he really had no idea what was up.

"Just trust me on this," said Agatha strongly. "This is going to work." She looked at her chalkboard and reveled in every mark. "The plan is perfect. We're going to kidnap Santa, and the do-goody fairy-tale heroes are going to give us the endings of their stories. I know it."

The laughter started as sniggering, then moved to guffawing, then turned into a bout of full-blown fiendish har-de-har howling. For the next few minutes, the Clandestines held their sides and laughed until they almost passed out. The villainous giggling, punctuated by a few snorts and more than one hiccup, echoed through the Abominable Snowman Café and into the street, where it terrified some and made a few others laugh.

Back inside, the lateness of the hour and the sour eggnog had made them punchy.

The Giant jumped up from his stools, hitting his head on the ceiling. "After we change the endings of the stories, I'm going to get me a Jack-and-cheese sandwich!"

Agatha held her sides and laughed. "And hold the beanstalks, eh, Giant?"

"Ha, ha, haaaarrr! I never eat my vegetables." As the Giant laughed, a snot bubble blossomed from his nose, which made him laugh even harder.

Grabbing great breaths between laughs, Medoza blurted out, "I'm going to stay up late and make Sleeping Beauty go to bed early *forever*!"

The Drama Queen chimed in next. "When Snow White is back asleep in the glass coffin, I'm going to make sure everyone can see her drooling, not to mention her terrible bed head!" The queen laughed so hard and shouted so loud she spit little white flecks all over the table.

Each wicked imagining inspired yet another, and another, and another, until those thoughts went round and round in the villains' heads like a diabolical yet catchy tune that just wouldn't go away.

When the laughter finally died down a bit, the queen scraped off the sludge-covered piano sitting in the corner of the café and uproariously belted out a favorite tune of the villains.

Just getting even just evens the score
Revenge is much sweeter because we get
more and more and more

The giant joined in on the chorus:

Sweet, sweet, sweet, sweet, sweet
REVENGE!

Medoza added in a loud voice,

We repeat, nothing can beat, good old,
sweet REVENGE!

When Agatha finally joined in, they repeated the chorus and cackled with sinister glee. They burst out the bottles of thistleweed tea. Then, as all raised their glasses, Agatha toasted, "To the happiness that we deserve. May everyone else be entirely miserable! Here's to good old . . ."

"To good old sweet REVENGE!" the whole crew cried out in one last Clandestine cackle.

CHAPTER 3

So Much Good in the World

MEANWHILE, on the other side of the North Pole, NPERLA had called a meeting where all could share their grievances about the workload they'd been under since Mother's Day. Goldman snuck in the back door just as Santa walked to the podium.

"Ho ho ho, hello, everyone," the jolly old man said with a smile. "I'm so glad you could all come.

I'd like to especially thank the North Pole Elf and Reindeer Labor Association for arranging this meeting and for providing the punch and cookies at the back."

Everyone in the room turned and looked at Goldman, who happened to be standing next to the refreshment table. He blushed and ducked into an empty seat.

"Now, I understand there are some concerns about Christmas this year," Santa said. "Please feel free to share them." He smiled and patted his round belly.

Hands went up all over the place.

"Santa, why are we making so many toys?"

"We haven't had a day off in months!"

"We've got the reindeer working the assembly lines and they don't even have thumbs!"

"Santa, I think the sleigh is too small."

One resourceful young elf with flaming red hair, small pointed ears, and a smattering of freckles stood up. Goldman tried not to stare. He knew her name already, the lovely Miss Imogene Butternut. She ran Santa's day-care playground for elf children age three to seven. She had a smile that blazed like the sun and a laugh that was contagious. He'd noticed her the first day he'd snuck in to Santa's workshop, and he'd quickly developed such a delirious crush on her that he impulsively spun a magnificent gold necklace for her from the straw in the reindeer stalls. Luckily, he came to his senses just before he gave it to her. He'd tried *not* to notice her ever since. It was difficult, though, because her voice sounded like birdsong and she smelled like sugar cookies. Gross—or was it?

Goldman shook himself out of whatever stupor he'd fallen into and forced himself to concentrate on what she was saying.

"Santa, is it true you said you were planning to haul toys from Singapore to Bangladesh without a break in Marrakesh, and with twice as many stops in North Korea and Vietnam?"

"Yeah, Santa!" someone else shouted. "What's going on? What's with all the toys?"

"Well, ho ho ho! These are all great questions and comments, elves," Santa said with a twinkle in his eye. "This year we're going to do things a little differently. This year is going to be special." All the elves leaned in close and held their breath. "This year we're going to give a toy to *every* child in the world!"

The elves sat in stunned silence. They were dumbfounded. Even Goldman was surprised.

"Wait. You can't mean that!" The leader of the elves' union stood up, his small fists clenched at his sides. "I must have heard you wrong. You can't possibly mean you're giving toys to the *naughty* kids as well?"

Santa smiled. "Yes, I do mean that, Reginald. I mean to give every child on the face of the earth a gift this year and every year hereafter."

"But . . . but . . . Santa!" Reginald sputtered. "What you're proposing would redefine our gift-giving tradition forever! What about the naughty-and-nice list? What about 'you better watch out'? Why, Santa? Why would you do this?" There was a murmur of concern throughout the room.

Santa took a deep breath. He knew his next words were going to be the most important, so he chose them carefully, hoping he'd be able to help his elves understand his vision. "I've been thinking lately about the whole reason behind giving gifts, and I believe we're missing our chance to change the world. What if, in addition to rewarding children for being good, we try investing in children who have the potential for being good but who need someone to believe that they *can* be good? What if the one toy we bring them encourages that goodness to come out in the open? What if I'm right in believing there is so much good in the world? And what if this little act of faith and love inspires kids to be as good as they never knew they could be? Wouldn't it be worth it then?"

The room fell silent once again. With mouths

open and heads shaking, the elves looked at each other. It was like Santa had just told them that children preferred a sweater from Aunt Carol to a cool new video game under the tree. There was no way they could have heard him right.

Goldman was starting to feel nauseated. All this talk of love and second chances sounded like a line to him. Ever since losing his fairy-tale ending years back, Goldman had lost all hope at a second chance for a family. From the moment the king's peasant bride had called out his true name, he'd realized he was too ugly and too short to love and too easy to betray. He'd give it another minute or two, then he'd slip out and have himself some skunk jerky. That always made him feel better.

One brave elf stepped forward. "Santa? There must be something strange in your cocoa." A ripple of nervous laughter rolled through the room. "You've always made a list and checked it twice. If you give toys to the naughty kids, won't the nice kids give up on trying to do what's right? I mean, where's the incentive?"

Santa curled a finger underneath his chin and nodded. "I see your point, Larry. We've always done it that way. But lately I've been wondering what would happen if instead of threatening children with a sack of coal, we give each and every one of them a gift—something that would inspire them. Nobody's perfect in every moment. Every kid tries to be good. Some just have a harder time than others. Maybe the greatest good some kids will do is still waiting deep inside them, somewhere. And maybe the gift we give this Christmas will turn them around and open their hearts.

You see, there is so much good in the world, my friends. We just need to encourage it to come out."

A room full of silent, wide-eyed elves looked back at Santa, and then someone started clapping. From the back of the room, one lone elf with lopsided ears clapped away until someone else joined him. Then another and another and another joined in. The applause grew slowly at first, but then it swelled in support of Santa's bold new direction for Christmas.

"Let's do it, Santa!" someone shouted.

"Let's find the good in everyone," another added.

Santa smiled as they cheered and clapped. "I'm so glad to hear you say that." His voice boomed above the noise. "Now, the clock is ticking. Let's get back to it, shall we? We have a lot of work to get done before Christmas Eve!"

They all cheered again. Goldman continued clapping until his gnarly little hands hurt. He was about to stop when he felt someone watching him. He turned his head and found the cute little red-headed Imogene smiling at him. She knew he'd been the first one to clap, and he could see the adoration in her eyes. He tried to ignore her but couldn't. He'd only started clapping to protect his cover, though he'd really hoped it would shut Santa up, because all his droning on about goodness was making Goldman sick. Funny thing, though . . . instead of his undercover semi-scowl, which he worked very hard to maintain, Goldman's lips twisted up, surprising him. He couldn't remember the last time he'd smiled, and the pull on his lips felt strange. Was all the sappy goodwill in the workshop beginning to rub off on him? Was he suffering from overexposure? Goldman shuddered to think of all that could come from a serious "goodness" infection, and he desperately wanted to find a dark closet to hide in, somewhere he could think nasty thoughts and shake off this dumb smile. He looked at the floor and quickly made his way out the door, repeating, "Smiles are for losers," over and over again, in spite of the grin he couldn't wipe off his face.

A Singing Telegram
for Santa

IT HAD TAKEN THE VILLAINS longer to get up to Santa's workshop than they had anticipated. First, the bus had broken down, and then the taxi had gotten lost. When the Drama Queen finally spelled up a broom, it wasn't big enough for all of them, especially the Giant. They ended up catching a ride with a herd of wild reindeer who weren't affiliated with Santa and who happened to be in the neighborhood visiting their reindeer relatives. It turned out to be a good thing for a couple of reasons. First, a flying reindeer could hold up to one hundred times its own weight, which made carrying the Giant possible, albeit a little awkward. And second, the skies over the North Pole workshop weren't guarded by protection spells, so the villains were able to literally drop in undetected.

The tension sizzled among the villains, now hunched in the bushes outside the workshop door. This was the Drama Queen's moment, and for a woman so passionate about musicals, every note counted. Much was riding on her performance as Telegram Stan. Since she was originating this role, she took a small measure of comfort in the fact that she wouldn't be compared to any other performer. But she knew if she messed up, all their plans for changing the endings of their stories would be for naught.

"Okay, everyone," Agatha whispered. "Do you have your costumes on?"

The Drama Queen's show included Telegram Stan's band. She wouldn't be able to sing without a band backing her up. So everyone, in disguise, was assigned an instrument: the Giant on tuba, Medoza on banjo, and Agatha on accordion with drums strapped to her back. Right before they went in, Mendoza would cast a spell that would shrink herself and her fellow band members to fit in a small suitcase, which the Drama Queen would carry into the workshop as Telegram Stan. Once inside the workshop, the suitcase would open up, the band would pop out, turning back into full-size imposters, and Stan would have a backup band. Not only that, but the Drama Queen would have real backup protection if she needed it. At the moment, however, they were more concerned with their wardrobe than with being at Santa's workshop.

"How does my wig look?" Medoza asked. In costume, she was a skinny man in his early twenties with acne scars, bleached-out hair, and sprayed-on pants.

"Who cares about your wig," the Drama Queen snapped. "What about my costume? Can you see my real clothes poking out anywhere? It feels like my dress keeps slipping out."

"You look fine," Agatha said. "What about me?" Her disguise made her look like a middle-aged, heavy-set balding man with droopy eyes.

The Giant's costume was the most complex.

In order for this to work, Medoza had needed to place a second spell on him to make sure he remained the size of a regular-sized man after he popped out of the suitcase. Double spells were risky, as they sometimes cancelled each other out without warning. Still, Medoza felt confident she could keep Giant's disguise under control. A small man now, he sported a pudding-bowl haircut and wore a smart little suit.

But the Drama Queen's costume was the best of all. She conjured up a fitted burgundy suit coat with a short collar and lined with gold buttons. A pair of big black enchanted pants hid her dress quite nicely. And on her head, a circular pillbox hat hid her waves and waves of black hair. It was the perfect disguise.

"You got this," Agatha whispered. "Break a leg."

"Yeah, grind your bones too!" The Giant laughed until Medoza elbowed him in the ribs.

"Ignore him," Medoza hissed. "Let's get this done."

In a poof of purple smoke, Agatha, Medoza, and the Giant disappeared into the small travel case. The Drama Queen snapped it shut, took a deep breath, and pulled her Mirror Mirror—travel size, of course—from the pocket of her plus-size pants.

"Mirror, Mirror, in my hand. How's my look as Telegram Stan?"

The mirror answered, "Imperfect as your rhyme may be, your clever disguise looks perfect to me."

It was all the reassurance she needed.

Calling from outside the door of Santa's

workshop, the Drama Queen deepened her voice as best she could and shouted, "Singing telegram for Santa! Singing telegram for Santa!"

Inside the workshop, all sounds of chatter and merriment stopped. The door opened and a rosy-cheeked Santa stepped out.

"Well, ho ho ho! A singing telegram for me? Why, I've never received such a thing. You came all the way to the North Pole to sing to me?"

Disguised as Telegram Stan, the Drama Queen smiled and opened her arms dramatically. "Yes, Santa Claus! I've come directly from Cinderella's castle. It was a long journey, so I hope I remember the whole telegram."

She set her small suitcase down next to her feet.

"What have you got here?" Santa asked as she flipped open the clasps on the suitcase.

"Oh, this?" she asked and smiled. "It's just my band. Hit it, guys!"

In another puff of purple smoke, the band appeared. And in less time than it takes to snap your fingers three times, they were ready to play.

This was it—the Drama Queen's big moment. She opened her mouth and began to sing.

> *Santa Claus! Santa Claus!*
> *Cinderella's having a party because*
> *Her fairy-tale friends all love you so!*
> *She's invited Snow White and the Seven*
> *   Dwarfs,*
> *Sleeping Beauty's going to be there, of*
> *   course.*
> *With Jack Anthebeanstalk and Pinocchio!*
> *They have got a gift for you,*
> *And they think you'll love it too.*

It's a super-duper, brand-new sleigh to
carry all your toys!
Santa Claus! Santa Claus!
Cinderella's having a party because
Her fairy-tale friends all love you so!

Santa loved it. She could tell. He clapped and smiled and tapped his feet along with the catchy, if somewhat off-key, tune.

The elves, however, were another story. Not one of them tapped a toe or shimmied a hip. They all stood with their arms folded and their eyes wary. When she'd finished singing, one rather obnoxious elf stepped forward.

"Santa, we don't have time for this. We're so busy as it is. If you leave, it's going to put us behind. You don't have time for a party. Tomorrow's Christmas Eve! You can't leave now!"

"Yeah," the others chimed in. "You can't leave now!"

The Drama Queen glared at the elves, but before she could say anything, Santa stepped forward.

"Now, settle down, all of you. You all know what we're up against this Christmas. A new sleigh is exactly what we need. Besides, it was very kind of Cinderella to invite me. It would be rude not to show up."

The elves began to list all the things that could happen if Santa left. Some were valid, like toys not getting made. Some were just silly, like one elf who said he just couldn't work if he didn't hear Santa's laugh. The Drama Queen started to panic. This was getting out of hand. She needed to do something. They were stealing her thunder. Worse yet, they were starting to convince Santa that going to the party was a bad idea.

Meanwhile, Medoza kept hearing the seams of the Giant's suit beginning to rip. His disguise spell was literally wearing off! She kept sending charm after charm to keep the Giant from bursting out of his suit, but her spells were getting weaker by the second.

Then the Drama Queen cued them to start playing the second verse. She began to sing at the top of her lungs, which just caused the elves to start shouting. In a moment, no one could hear anything.

A sharp whistle pierced the noise, and Santa held up his hands. The band ceased playing, and Telegram Stan ended on a high note that made everyone in the room grimace. The Drama Queen smiled smugly to herself. Silence settled over the workshop.

The Drama Queen cleared her throat. "What shall I tell Cinderella, Santa? Will you be attending?"

Santa didn't wait a second before he answered. "Of course. Tell Cinderella and all her guests I'd be happy to come." The elves continued to protest, but Santa held up his finger. "But also tell her that I can't stay long. This is my busiest time of year. She'll understand that."

"Of course," the Drama Queen answered as she tried not to smile too wickedly. "I'll tell everyone you're coming. Have a safe trip!" Medoza was sweating so much trying to hold all the spells together that her wig was beginning to look like a soaking wet mop. Somehow she managed to conjure one more puff of purple smoke to shrink the band back into the suitcase, and the Drama Queen sealed them up beneath the clasps. Leaving the suitcase on the ground by her feet, she withdrew a scroll from her pocket and handed it to Santa. "Here. Before I forget," she said.

Santa took it, his eyebrows raised. "What is this?"

She started to tell him it was the plans for the sleigh, but she noticed that her dress was starting to poke out of her disguise. She could feel her magic slipping.

Stay calm, she told herself. *Keep in character.*

"A present," she said as she carefully began to walk toward the door, making sure to keep her hands wrapped tightly around her enchanted pants

lest they magically disappear and give her true identity away.

"Wait," a voice from the crowd called out.

Afraid to look, she turned and ran for the door. An elf caught up to her, his wrinkled hands and face familiar.

Goldman.

"You forgot your suitcase, *Stan*," the elf said with a wink.

"Thanks," she whispered, and she slipped out the door without a second glance.

The suitcase in the Drama Queen's hand was getting heavier with every step. She had to get clear of the workshop as fast as possible. By the time she crossed Main Street, just barely out of view from the workshop, she was dragging the suitcase behind her. She ducked into an alleyway behind an old marshmallow factory and snapped open the suitcase claps. Exploding out of the case and returning to her normal form, Medoza struggled to catch her breath. "Are you kidding me," she gasped. "What would have happened if you'd forgotten the suitcase? I was barely holding on in there!"

"Calm down," said the Drama Queen defensively. "I got us out, didn't I?"

"Yes! But that was too close!" said Agatha with authority. "Now pull yourselves together, ladies. We can't afford to make any more mistakes."

The Giant's stomach began to rumble like thunder. "I'm getting hungry," he said.

"It won't be long now, Giant," Agatha said with a sinister grin. "It won't be long now."

CHAPTER 5

It's a Dream Sleigh

INCLUDING PLANS FOR Santa's new sleigh as part of the ruse had been Agatha's idea. Because she knew a guy who knew a guy who owed her a favor who also turned out to be great with forgeries, she ended up with drawings for the most amazing reindeer sleigh ever imagined. It was a brilliant mishmash of cars, airplanes, space shuttles, helicopters, and the finest tour buses of Nashville's biggest country music stars. So the moment Santa unrolled the scroll Telegram Stan had handed him, his eyes widened, his heart skipped a beat, and he gasped for air.

"Elves! Great sticky buns! Elves! Sweet jingle bells! This is the answer to all our problems!"

Santa held the drawings of the sleigh with a reverence reserved for precious documents like the Declaration of Independence . . . or Santa's favorite peanut-butter-bar recipe. The beauty and complexity of the mechanics alone almost made him cry.

"It's a dream sleigh," he told the elves. "Just look at this. What you see defines my bliss!"

"Uh-oh." One of the elves shook his head. "Here he goes again."

It was a well-known, documented fact around the North Pole that when Santa got excited he

began speaking in rhyme. No one knew why, not even Santa himself, but the elves had learned to go with it, and in this instance, they couldn't blame him. The design of the sleigh was pure poetry.

Santa held the plans up to the light for a better look. "In every detail . . . the look and feel. I can't believe this dream is real."

His eyes glazed over and he wandered out of the workshop and onto the snow-covered path toward the barn where his reindeer lived.

Dasher and Dancer were enjoying a dinner of barley and oats when Santa and his elves strolled in through the barn doors. He hurried over to their stalls and held up the sketches.

"Can you see this, my friends? This is a dream sleigh with custom chrome. A mobile home away from home!"

The two reindeer looked at each other as if to say, "I told you this day would come. He's loooos-ing it."

Santa didn't even notice. "It's aerodynamic, with so much torque, and yet it will handle like a Porsche."

One of the younger elves leaned close to one of his elders. "Did he just rhyme *torque* with *Porsche*?"

The older elf hushed him. "It's best if you don't say anything and just go with it."

Santa reached a stack of hay bales, where he spread out the plans so everyone could see them. They showed that every safety test had been soundly aced and that the sleigh could move at a light-speed pace with total ease and grace. But even as they read the specs, some began to feel that something was wrong with this picture—not the actual sketches themselves; they were perfect—but you know what they say about things that seem too good to be true. The elves were skeptical. Something didn't feel right.

Oblivious to the suspicions around him, Santa's eyes devoured the images in front of him. Then, with a shout of joy that could be heard from the North Pole to Norway, Santa exclaimed, "Will you take a look at all the cargo space!"

One would have thought angelic choirs had begun to sing with the way Santa danced around the barn. His rosy red cheeks seemed even more so, and his eyes had countless twinkles. He started to laugh when he noticed that the wood trim was bamboo. Then he shouted that the engine was eco-friendly too because it was powered by reindeer poop. And finally, at the top of his voice, he thanked the universe that all his dreams were coming true with this super, totally brand-new reindeer hybrid sleigh!

Every child was going to get a toy this year, and Santa had to go to Cinderella's Christmas Eve party to thank her in person.

Santa tucked the plans into his pocket and turned to look at those who had followed him to the barn. "Elves! Saddle up Rudolph, and load a sack of gifts for the party guests. I'll be back before you know it with a sleigh that can help us deliver a toy to every child in the world this year. We're going to change the world by finding the good in everyone. I just know it!"

The elves watched as Santa and Rudolph flew off over the horizon. Christmas Eve had arrived, and they wondered what the day would bring.

CHAPTER 6

Surprise Parties

WHILE AGATHA AND her evil friends were making final preparations to kidnap Santa, Cinderella's Christmas party was just starting. Set on a beautiful hillside, the enchanted fairy-tale castle had been decorated in ribbons and light. Inside, the adornments of the season abounded. Christmas trees of all sizes filled every nook and cranny, some large enough to

reach the vaulted ceiling and some so small they had to be set on tabletops. Wreaths and lights, candles and candy canes celebrated the season. Boxes wrapped in bright paper and tied with gold ribbons sat in decorative stacks beneath the trees. It was the ultimate Christmas Eve celebration, and the guests had just started to arrive.

A smartly dressed herald who also happened to be named Harold stood by the door and announced the arrivals while his buddies sounded the trumpets. A few years ago, the Fairy Tale Party Planning Committee had forwarded a motion to replace the trumpets with a rock guitar and the chamber orchestra with a DJ—move the party into the twenty-first century, so to speak—but the idea was defeated by a vote of twenty-eight to two (the two coming from the guitar player's wife and the DJ, of course).

In the world of fairy tales, tradition rules.

As the sun set on a beautifully clear Christmas Eve, the trumpets sounded and the booming voice of Harold the herald shouted, "Announcing Sleeping Beauty and Prince Fillmore!"

Inside the castle, a long gilded staircase led to the ballroom where everyone was gathering before dinner. Looking beautiful in her periwinkle gown, Cinderella stood next to Prince Charming at the bottom-most stair in order to greet everyone as they arrived.

"Oh, Sleeping Beauty! I'm so glad you could come." Cinderella smiled at her friend as they exchanged dainty air kisses.

"Thank you for having me. And remember, it's

Nora. I'm trying to put all those sleeping days behind me." She smiled. "I'm wide awake now. You
remember my husband?"

"Of course," Cinderella said. "We're indebted
to you for waking up our dear friend."

A blush crossed Prince Fillmore's face and disappeared into his brown hair. "I made brownies,"
he said as he tried to balance a china plate and
hold on to Nora's hand at the same time. "They're
a little burned around the edges, though."

"Are you kidding? That's the best part."
Cinderella smiled as a servant swooped in and took
the plate from Fillmore before he could drop it.

"I know how it is," Prince Charming stepped
up. "You can save the girl from the fire-breathing
dragon, but don't ask us to cook, right?"

"Right." The two men laughed.

Any further conversation was interrupted when the trumpets blared and Harold announced, "Beauty and the Beast . . . er . . . I mean, Prince Andrew." Harold gratefully stepped back into the shadows.

If Beauty had noticed the slip up, she didn't let on. Instead, she flew down the staircase with a smile on her face, her beautiful yellow gown swirling behind her.

"Nora! Cindy! It's been too long. You both look gorgeous, as always."

The three women hugged as best they could without messing up their hair or their dresses. Cinderella stepped away but held on to her friends' hands. "I'm sorry I missed book club this week. What with the party and all, I had so much to organize. Good thing I got all the woodland creatures to help."

Next to her, Prince Charming rolled his eyes. "Help? You ought to see the mess *they* make," he mumbled.

Fillmore laughed.

"You didn't really miss anything," Nora said, elbowing Fillmore. "It was *Rip Van Winkle.* We pretty much slept through the review."

A third man joined the group. Young and handsome, he didn't look anything like the hairy beast he'd been when Beauty had first come to know him. But as it always is in fairy tales, love triumphed and his curse had been broken. Prince Andrew stood before them, as perfect as a man could be.

Prince Charming shook Prince Andrew's hand

and told him how glad he was to see him. Fillmore nodded and agreed.

The trumpets sounded once again and another announcement was made: "Snow White and Prince Francis!"

The group at the bottom of the stairs beamed as the woman with creamy white skin and rose-red lips joined them.

"Thank you for inviting us," Snow White said. "We love coming to your Christmas Eve party. It's always so relaxing!"

The ladies huddled around Snow White and cooed about dresses and hair and perfect skin.

"What's your secret?" Beauty asked.

Snow brushed at her ebony hair. "I try to stay out of the sun," she said. "And I've been using this new magic face cream I bought off an old woman I met in the forest. I'll tell you all about it."

The princes rolled their eyes and began talking about hunting dragons and other more manly activities.

The trumpets sounded for the last time as Pinocchio and Geppetto, along with Jack Anthebeanstalk, entered.

The group of princes and princesses met them at the bottom of the staircase, where more hugging and kissing ensued.

"Why, Pinocchio, you look wonderful! It's always so nice to see you as a real boy these days and not as a wooden puppet," Cinderella said.

Geppetto smiled and stood a little taller. "I'm a-so proud of him; he's a-such a good boy."

Geppetto's Italian accent rolled his words around in a singsong manner.

"Gee, Cinderella, thanks for asking us to your par—" Pinocchio's new boy legs wobbled and he tipped into a sea of satin, tulle, and lace. "Whoa! Oh boy! I'm sorry."

"That's all right, Pinocchio. Everyone trips sometimes," Cinderella said as Prince Charming picked him up and made sure he was steady on his feet before letting him go.

The group greeted Jack, who'd brought a beanstalk soufflé that had, unfortunately, deflated on the ride over. He wondered aloud if he should have made deviled eggs instead. Then again, however flat it was, his soufflé *was* made from the eggs of his golden goose, so at the very least he knew it would be delicious.

A servant came and took the flattened soufflé from Jack, directing everyone to the dining room, where a table as long as a football field sat laden with all kinds of mouthwatering dishes.

Slow-roasted pork shoulder with mustard and sage sat next to a platter of braised brisket. Spicy hot chocolate and baked French toast with pecan crumbles shared a space with sea-salt caramels and chewy molasses cookies. Turkey with piles of stuffing and potatoes mingled with honey-cured ham and candied carrots. There was even a roast beast piled among the baked yams. It was a feast fit for a king.

Cinderella couldn't have been more pleased. "Everyone, may I have your attention please?" The room quieted down as all eyes turned to her. "We are so glad you could all make it to our kingdom's

annual Christmas Eve party. Let's get this party officially underway with dinner. It's buffet style, so fill your plates and enjoy the conversation around you. Tonight, *nuestra* castle *es su* castle."

Everyone smiled and clapped politely as they eyeballed the delicious food. Music from the orchestra began playing, and everyone flocked to the buffet table. It was shortly after everyone had filled their plates and sat down that a few of them thought they heard the faint sound of sleigh bells. Thinking that it was just part of the party, they continued on with dinner.

A moment later, there came a knock at the massive front door.

Cinderella turned to Harold, who was stuffing his mouth with a succulent turkey leg.

"Are we expecting anyone else?" she asked.

His eyebrows furrowed and he shook his head as he swallowed. "No, m'lady. Everyone on the invite list has arrived."

Cinderella looked confused. "Go let them in!"

Harold jumped up from the table and raced out of the room. When the rest of the guests heard that someone was at the door, they all pushed away from the table and joined Cinderella at the bottom of the large gilded staircase.

Much to their surprise, it was Santa Claus who stepped in when the massive doors opened.

Cinderella's jaw dropped open. "Santa! What are you doing here? It's Christmas Eve!"

"Ho ho ho! Merry Christmas Eve, fairy-tale friends. I know it's late, and I can't stay long, but thank you so much for inviting me. I'm thrilled, and of course, I've brought presents." And out of the large red sack he'd brought from the North Pole, a pile of brightly wrapped gifts appeared, each labeled with the name of someone in attendance. The group oohed and aahed.

Cinderella pressed her hands to her cheeks and said, "That is so very kind of you, Santa. We know you're so busy. Did you say you had an invitation?" She looked over at Harold, who discreetly shook his head.

"Yes, of course," Santa replied as he pulled the fake invitation from his pocket. "Please, let me tell you all how grateful I am for the new super-duper reindeer hybrid sleigh. It's almost like you knew exactly what I needed this year. You see, I'm giving a toy to every girl and boy in the world, and my old sleigh just can't handle that kind of volume. I can't tell you how much this gift means to me and the elves. It is truly a blessing!"

Prince Charming joined Cinderella, and a confused look passed between them as a surprised silence settled over the palace. Near the back of the crowd, an awkward cough or two echoed off the ceiling. Somewhere off to the side, a cricket chirped.

"Hush," Pinocchio whispered loudly. "Nobody knows why he's here."

Cinderella stepped forward and took Santa's hands in her own. "Santa, we're so happy you joined us, but I don't remember sending you an invitation. You're welcome to stay, of course, but we figured you'd be busy, what with it being Christmas Eve and all . . ."

Santa laughed and his belly jiggled like a bowl

full of jelly. "You are so right, my dear. It wasn't just an invitation. It was a singing telegram. And a funny-looking one at that."

Cinderella looked back at Prince Charming, who shook his head in confusion.

"A singing telegram, Santa?"

Santa raised an eyebrow. "He had a band too. Telegram Stan's band, he called them." He looked around at the fairy-tale characters gathered, and a small suspicion began to build in the pit of his stomach. "You never sent a singing telegram, did you?" It wasn't a question.

Cinderella shook her head. "No, Santa. We assumed you'd be busy. It is Christmas Eve," she said again.

Santa's brow furrowed. "Who would have sent it, then? Who would have sent me an invitation and . . . these sleigh drawings?" He held out his hand, his fingers curled around the rolled sketches.

Right then, a crash of light and a puff of purple smoke erupted from the sketches. Santa dropped them at his feet, and the crowd gasped and moved back. The pictures of the super hybrid sleigh faded until the papers were blank.

A moment later, in bloodred ink, the words, "HA, HA, HA, HA, HA!" appeared on one of the pages, only to be followed by the hideous sound of sinister laughter. A ball of flames and a burst of thunder blew the front door open, and in walked the Clandestines!

They all moved quickly into the castle, except for Goldman, who had stayed behind at the North Pole, monitoring the elves just in case the Clandestines needed to use their backup plan.

They took their positions surrounding Santa Claus, and a cry of fear arose inside the palace.

Cinderella gasped. "Stepmother!"

"Surprise, goodie-goodie stepdaughter!" Agatha laughed fiendishly. "You really need to work out the bugs in your security, my dear!"

"What are you doing here?" Cinderella cried.

"You'll find out soon enough," Agatha answered.

Medoza took her magic staff and, with a whirl, began to cast an evil spell. Before anyone could move, a swirl of black smoke surrounded Santa Claus. He tried to run but found that his hands were stuck at his sides and that he couldn't move a toe or even an eyelash.

"What are you doing?" Beauty cried as she pushed to the front of the crowd.

The Giant grabbed her before she could get near Santa and yanked her away. In horror, everyone watched as Santa swirled in a cyclone of magic dust, shrinking to the size of a small figurine. As the swirls of black smoke faded away, the party guests quickly discovered that Medoza had imprisoned Santa in a snow globe!

"What have you done?" Cinderella breathed in horror. Her knees felt weak, and she could feel the tears pushing from behind her eyes.

From inside the globe, Santa struggled against the glass, but the enchanted globe held him fast.

Medoza answered as she scooped the tiny prison from off the floor. "Oh, it's simple, dearies. We have something you want, and you have something we want. So we'd like to make a little trade."

"What kind of trade?" Jack questioned, being

careful to stay away from the Giant, who still had a hold on Beauty.

Medoza laughed at him. Jack tried to grab the globe from her but she shook it in his face, then snatched it away. "I don't think so, Jack. We put a spell on Santa, and we're going to keep him locked safely inside until . . ."

"Until what?" Snow White implored.

The Clandestines grinned at each other, then Medoza said, "Until every one of you agrees to let us change the endings to all of our fairy tales. Every one of them!"

A gasp of shock radiated through the large room as everyone stared, wide-eyed, at each other. Was this for real? Did they really mean it?

Seeing the looks on their faces made the Drama Queen laugh. She stepped forward and came toe-to-toe with Snow White. "Oh yes, we're serious. It's time we got the last laugh. We will release Santa Claus if you eat the poisoned apple."

"No!" Prince Francis shouted as he tried to push through the crowd.

Medoza walked over to Nora and looked the princess straight in the eye. "And you, my dear, have a date with a spinning wheel. You're going to sleep forever." Her laughter filled the vaulted ceiling, along with more shouts of protest.

Over in the corner, the Giant smashed one of his fists into the other with a terrifying crack. "You guys always win." He glared at Beauty, who shuddered. "Every time someone reads a fairy tale, we end up the losers." He pulled out his knife and fork and tied on a bib. "I'm going to finally get my Jack-and-cheese sandwich. Heh-heh-heh." He began to drool.

Jack ducked back into the crowd.

Agatha looked over at Cinderella, who watched her with fearful eyes. "Oh yes, and that's just the beginning. Beauty's handsome prince will go back to being a beast. Pinocchio will live out the rest of his days as a wooden boy. And dear Cinderella, you'll return to being my slave. You'll work until that mess of a castle is spotless, and then you'll start all over again. Forever." Prince Charming opened his mouth to argue, but Agatha silenced him with a venomous look. "Agree to all that, and we'll let Santa go."

Cinderella spoke for all her friends when she said, "This is terrible. Just terrible!"

"Why, thank you," Agatha sneered. "We feel

perfectly rotten about it ourselves." The Clandestines' fiendish cackles rolled through the palace, causing a shiver to run down the spines of the fairy-tale friends.

The Giant smacked his lips and looked hungrily at Jack.

"This isn't right!"

The small voice came from the back of the room. "You realize that by kidnapping Santa you've pretty much destroyed Christmas. How can you do that to the children of the world?" Pinocchio pushed his way to the front of the crowd. "I know I haven't had a real boy brain for long, but I don't understand how you can be so awful. Why would you do this?"

The Drama Queen narrowed her eyes as she looked down at the small boy. Tiny dimples graced his cheeks and his hair swirled into a charming cowlick that curled over his forehead, making him look sweet and innocent, a look that made her sicker than usual.

"Revenge, you naïve little boy. Sweet, sweet revenge! Like the Giant says, we're sick of losing in the end. Now it's *our* turn to write the ends of the stories."

Pinocchio looked over at the small snow globe clutched in Medoza's hand and at the jolly old elf trapped inside. Even in this most dire of circumstances, Santa Claus still wore his characteristic smile. In fact, one of his twinkling eyes looked over at Pinocchio and *winked*. Pinocchio watched with amazement as Santa Claus pulled something out of his pocket, something that looked a lot like a pocketknife, and set whatever it was up against the glass. Pinocchio began to smile too as he anticipated Santa's escape.

Perhaps it was the innocent wish-upon-a-star belief of a wooden puppet turned real boy, or maybe it was a defect in the magical globe, but a sudden explosion of light caused everyone, including the Clandestines, to fall back and cover their eyes.

The explosion was followed by a crash, which ended with a boom.

With wide eyes, everyone watched as the snow globe released Santa from his prison. He landed nimbly on the floor and quickly began to swell back to normal size. The fairy-tale friends cheered as Santa returned to them.

The Clandestines were stumped.

"Ho ho ho! Well, that was quite the adventure."

Santa stretched his gloved hands above his head and turned to look at his captors. "You realize I've never had a problem with locked doors, right? I've always been a chimney man, and a snow globe is sort of like a chimney in that neither one of them has very much space." He uncurled his fist and allowed those around him to see the tool lying in his palm.

Prince Charming stepped forward and said with a hint of awe in his voice, "Is that the brand-new, full-magic-charged army-man utility tool and laser cannon? I've been wanting one of those for months!"

"Why, yes, it is," Santa replied happily. "Mrs. Claus got it for me for Father's Day. I can never pull out the can opener, but the laser cannon works quite well."

On the ground, the prince could see tiny wisps of smoke curling up from the broken pieces of glass.

"That's brilliant," Prince Charming said.

"Oh, Santa," Pinocchio said as he ran up and hugged Santa. "I was so afraid Christmas would be ruined."

"Now, don't you worry about that, young man. I'd never let the children of the world down. I am too smart for that." His eyes twinkled. "But thank you for caring about old Santa." He pulled the little boy into a big hug.

"Ugh. I think I'm gonna be sick," the Drama Queen groaned.

"You and me both," Agatha agreed, then turned to Santa. "You may be too smart to stay locked up inside a snow globe, but you're not as smart as you think you are."

Prince Fillmore pushed his way up to his wife and pulled her into his arms. "What do you mean? Santa's loose. We don't have to give in to your demands."

"Don't be so sure." Medoza sniggered. "You see, evil always has a plan B. While you goodie-goodies were here stuffing your faces with holiday treats, our mole inside the North Pole arranged to have all the toys stolen from Santa's workshop. Every last one of them! He's hidden them where no one can find them. No one but us, that is."

The Clandestines began cackling again, the sound growing until it filled the room.

"What a horrible thing to do," Cinderella said, almost in tears.

"You want revenge bad enough to steal toys from children?" Beauty asked in disbelief.

"Yes. We do," the Drama Queen answered. "And if you give in to our demands, you can have all the toys back. Or you can disappoint all the girls and boys of the world. It's really your choice. We'll give you a few moments to think about it," she said. "But don't dawdle. It's only a few hours till Christmas morning."

With that, the Clandestines turned and hurried out the door they had blown off its hinges just a few minutes before with their explosive entrance.

• • •

Now, the true reason the villains were giving the friends a chance to think things over wasn't because they thought time would make any difference. The end result was going to be the same no matter how much time they took. They did it because they couldn't stand being inside the castle another minute. There was something about being around so much goodness (and for whatever reason there seemed to be a particularly concentrated dose in the castle) that was making them incredibly uncomfortable.

Goldman had warned them about the dangers of overexposure to a place with genuine love, where abundance was available for everyone and not just a few, but they hadn't really believed him until now. To their horror, the food in the castle was actually starting to smell delicious. The decorations were starting to look pretty. And even the glowing fireplaces started to seem inviting! They had to get out of there as soon as possible to remind themselves that all of those things were disgusting. Luckily Goldman had insisted that they at least carry a few emergency countermeasures in Agatha's knapsack. It had a few nose plugs, a small bag of rancid skunk jerky, and a bottle of Barnaby's thistleweed drink.

"Agatha, quick!" the Drama Queen groaned between clenched teeth. "I need a piece of that skunk jerky—I'm losing it!"

"Let's all keep calm," Agatha said as she passed around what precious little skunk jerky there was in the knapsack. She noticed that Medoza was struggling to catch her breath. "Come on, Medoza, drink some of the thistleweed drink."

"NO!" cried Medoza. "That stuff might taste disgusting to good people, but I think it might actually be healthy! Seriously, my skin and hair have been uncharacteristically glowing since I started drinking it. No more! Give me the real deal! Any poison-ivy chips in that knapsack?"

"No, Medoza," Agatha sneered. "Just take it easy and chew your skunk jerky . . . slowly." Then, looking at the Giant, who seemed to be holding his breath, she said, "You still with us, Giant?"

"Yeah," he said. "But I'm gonna need a nose plug. I don't want to smell that food again!"

Agatha pulled out a nose plug, and Medoza cast a quick spell on it to make it large enough to clamp over his massive nostrils. "All right, now listen," she said.

"Ooh. I call the jerky crumbs!" said the Drama Queen, grabbing the bag.

"No you don't." Medoza snatched it away from her. "You already had the biggest piece."

"Oh, yeah?" The Drama Queen pulled out her wand.

"Just try it, witch!" Medoza hissed.

"Stop it! Both of you," Agatha commanded.

Holding her thumb and finger close together, she said, "We are *this* close to getting what we want. Are you both going to lose it over a few crumbs of skunk jerky?"

The two women stopped fighting but glared at each other.

"That's better," Agatha said. "Now let's get back in there and finish this!"

The Giant kept mumbling something about how hungry he was.

"Surprise, surprise," Agatha said. "What else is new, Giant?" Chewing on her jerky, she confidently led the Clandestines back inside the castle.

CHAPTER 7

We Can't Go Back

WHILE THE VILLAINS WERE regrouping outside, the fairy-tale friends were still reeling from shock. With Santa back, they all gravitated to the dining room again where some sat, some stood, and some picked absently at the turkey leftovers, each dealing with the stress differently. It didn't take long before they began to talk about it.

"What a horrible situation," Snow White said. "I mean, it's good we got you back, Santa, but these demands are unreasonable. Change the endings of our stories? That would mean I'd have to be put back in that glass coffin." Her skin blanched even whiter than normal.

Prince Charming hurried over to her side and held her hands. "That's not going to happen, sweetheart. I promise."

"I'm not touching that spinning wheel again," Nora said. "You have no idea what kind of nightmares I had. The sleepwalking was horrible! I ended up in the royal pantry one night. I ate four red velvet cakes before someone found me. I won't do it again. I won't!"

Prince Fillmore wrapped his arms around her and swore that his love would be true forever, no matter how much she weighed or how often she walked in her sleep. It didn't make her feel better.

"Well, I have no desire to be changed into a beast again," Prince Andrew growled. "You have no idea what it's like to be stared at all the time. Or mocked and ridiculed every time you go out. Worse yet are the people who fear me. Do you know how many times angry mobs almost burned my castle down? No. I don't want to go back to that."

Beauty promised she'd never leave him, no matter what, but Andrew still couldn't wrap his mind around becoming a beast again.

"Yeah, well, at least you all won't end up as supper!" Jack said. "If my story changes, not only would I lose my cow, my goose, and my dad, but that giant out there gets to eat me! Where's the silver lining in that?"

"Fair point," a few of them mumbled.

"He might swallow you whole!" Pinocchio offered.

Cinderella trembled when she thought about how her world would consist of working her fingers to the bone, slaving away for her stepmother and two stepsisters. But it wasn't waiting on them hand and foot that she hated as much as it was the weekends. Since her ugly stepsisters were never asked out on dates, Cinderella would once again be commanded to play Uno with them for hours on end. "I think I'd rather have the Giant eat me," she said miserably.

But beneath those fears was an even greater one. What message would it send if the endings of their fairy tales were changed? What kind of damage would be done to the readers of fairy tales if, after all was said and done, evil triumphed over good? They had to consider the possibility that this could cause a literary catastrophe from which the world might never recover.

Pinocchio, the youngest member of the group, had been silent and respectful as the older and more experienced fairy-tale heroes shared their fears. During a break in the discussion, when it seemed that they had said all they had to say, Pinocchio stood up and walked to the front of the room.

Clearing his throat, he looked out over the group. "I promise you, I can't deny the joy I've known since I became a real boy. I don't want to be turned into a puppet any more than you don't want to go back to the lives you lived—or didn't live. But think about it. Santa is trying something this year that's never been done before. He's looking for the good in all children, not just some of them. If going back and rewriting the ends of our stories means that on this special Christmas day no child will be forgotten . . . well, it seems to me a small price to pay."

All of the fairy-tale friends took a moment to reflect on this. Then they thought about all the children who had heard their stories and cheered for them every time one of their stories was told. So much of their own happiness had come from those kids.

Pinocchio continued. "We all have so much at stake here, and maybe it's because I'm so young that all this seems clear to me, but I truly believe that most every person, when they're small, can't wait until they're tall. And only when they're grown do they learn that once they leave their childhood, they can't return. If Christmas doesn't come because of us, will the kids who might have had a chance to find the good in themselves this year find it any other way? Will we be responsible for taking this most precious Christmas away from them?"

The fairy-tale friends felt the truth in young Pinocchio's words and were humbled.

Even Jack agreed and said, "You know, stories come and stories go. We'll all find new ones as we grow, but childhood memories so sublime only happen once upon a time."

Cinderella added, "There is no gift from Santa and his elves as wonderful as giving of ourselves.

And even though it's hard for us to change our stories' end, we'll save what only happens once . . . because the children can't go back again."

"So we'll go back," said Beauty. "We'll take this on?"

Jack lifted his chin. "I don't want to be the one to stand in the way of any child finding goodness in the world."

"We might be giving the Clandestines our endings," added Snow White, "but we'll really be giving a beautiful fairy tale to every child in the world!"

Jack took a moment, then courageously said, "I'll change the ending of my story."

"So will I," Cinderella said.

"And I," Nora agreed.

All the others chimed in as well.

In the corner, Santa hadn't said a word. He'd just listened and smiled.

And so the decision was unanimous. They all agreed that Christmas had to happen, no matter what.

CHAPTER 8

On One Condition

HEN THE CLANDESTINES returned to the palace, they brought with them a very distinct odor that became more pungent by the minute.

Cinderella stepped forward to respond to her stepmother's demands, took a whiff, covered her nose, and took three steps back. "What in the world is that smell?" She felt her eyes begin to water.

"Skunk jerky," Agatha answered with a smile. "There's none for you, so don't ask."

Cinderella could see bits of it in Agatha's teeth and it turned her stomach.

"Oh, that's all right, Stepmother," she said as politely as she could, considering the circumstances.

"Well, what's your answer?" Agatha yelled impatiently. "We're running out of time!"

Cinderella gathered herself. "We've thought it over and we have decided . . . " She took a breath and looked over at her friends, who gave her an encouraging nod. "We've decided to accept your offer. Christmas must be saved, no matter what."

Before a cheer could erupt from the Clandestines, Santa interrupted.

"On one condition," he said in a firm but kind voice.

"What? No," Medoza said. "There are no conditions."

Santa's eyebrows shot up. "Is that so? Well, if you don't agree to my condition, then I won't be able to deliver Christmas and the fairy-tale friends are free to keep the endings of their stories."

Every jaw in the room dropped. The Clandestines looked at each other, but none had any kind of rebuttal.

"But, Santa," Cinderella protested. "You can't. The kids!"

He held up a finger for silence. "Do you agree to honor my condition?" he asked Medoza.

Her eyes narrowed. "What is it?" she sneered.

Santa smiled. "That you not only return all the gifts but also help us deliver them tonight."

The Clandestines looked at each other and started to laugh. "Are you being serious? Why should we help you deliver the toys?" the Drama Queen asked.

"Because of this plan of yours, Christmas Eve is almost over and I haven't even begun to get my delivery schedule started. Without help—your help—I'll never get the toys delivered on time."

"That's your problem," Agatha growled.

"Not quite." Santa laid it out like the closing argument at a trial. "Like I said before, it's your problem too. If we don't get those toys delivered before Christmas, you won't have anything to bargain with."

"But they already agreed!" the Giant barked, pointing at the fairy-tale friends.

"They agreed as long as you gave the presents back, but that would be meaningless unless Christmas gets delivered this year," Santa pointed out. "Christmas needs to be delivered tonight. If that doesn't happen, there is no bargain. The fairy-tale friends leave with the endings of their stories and you leave with nothing. Either help us deliver Christmas and rewrite the endings of your stories or walk away with nothing. It's your choice."

"He's right. I never thought about it that way," the Giant said.

"You never think at all," Medoza snapped.

"Hey! That's not nice," the Giant shot back.

"We don't do nice!" Medoza growled.

"Knock it off, you two," Agatha commanded. "I need to think about this."

Cinderella looked at her stepmother. "If you really want revenge, you're going to have to help us."

"And how do we know this isn't a trick?" Medoza wondered aloud.

"How do we know you'll let us change the endings if we do help?" the Drama Queen asked.

"Because that's the difference between you and us," Snow White said. "We keep our word. You can count on it."

"You have our promise," Nora said sincerely.

"To show our good faith," Pinocchio volunteered, "I will become a puppet while we deliver the toys together."

Then Prince Andrew stepped up. "And I'll become the ugly beast again."

"And I, Agatha, will become your servant after we help Santa deliver his toys," Cinderella added.

For a moment, the Clandestines didn't know what to say. They never in a million years had anticipated a response like this, so they mulled things over in a stinky huddle.

The Giant looked over the heads of everyone and found who he was looking for. "What will you do, Jack? Everyone else is doing something. I'm hungry. Gimme a taste. Just your baby toes."

"No way!" Jack backed away, glad his toes were safely covered in his boots.

"Then I'm not gonna help with the toys," the Giant said resolutely.

Santa stepped forward again. "Now, Giant,

Jack can't very well deliver toys without toes. That's not going to work. He's going to need them for the busy night ahead."

The Giant shook his head stubbornly. "No one needs their pinky toes."

Santa looked over at Jack, then winked. "Why don't you let him lick your arm or something, Jack? You know, as sort of a show of good faith."

"What? No. I . . ." Jack sputtered.

The Giant nodded. "Okay then, one lick."

"What do you think, Jack?" Santa asked as he discreetly looked at his watch. Everyone knew time was running out.

"Fine. I'll—" Before Jack could say another word he was blindsided and drenched by a giant tongue. "EEEWWW! YUCK!" Jack exclaimed. It was as if he'd been splashed by a hundred buckets of slime. It might have been the grossest thing to happen in fairy tale history!

Meanwhile, the Clandestines agreed that they really had no choice in the matter. They had to help Santa deliver the toys, and since it was only for one night, why not just get it over with as soon as possible?

CHAPTER 9

Logistical Nightmare or Dream Come True?

SANTA CLAUS HAD ALWAYS been a list maker. His to-do lists in preparing for Christmas Eve were even more legendary among his inner circle of friends than every list he'd ever made of the naughty and nice. Since he'd decided to give a toy to every child in the world, that list was absent this season, but it had been replaced by a last-minute list of all the challenges he now faced. It looked like this:

1. Kidnapped—running late!
2. Lots of toys—not a big enough sleigh!
3. Need to reload two or three times.
4. New delivery routes—check with air-traffic control.
5. Reindeer will need more food and rest stops.
6. New people on the job—some have "behavior" problems.
7. Breakage—mainly worried about the Giant.
8. Scared children—what if they wake up to find a witch in their house instead of Santa?

Could everyone come together and pull this off, or would it be the greatest nightmare in the history of Christmas Eve nights? The only way out of this mess, he reasoned, would be through it, so Santa rallied everyone back to the North Pole as quickly as he could.

One unexpected advantage to having the Clandestines on board was Drama Queen's unique access to the most up-to-date and intelligent Magic Mirror operating system in the world. Everyone delivering presents this Christmas Eve could refer to a handheld magic mirror for almost every question that might come up. The mirrors functioned better than any GPS device on the market and they were the most sophisticated mobile phones any of them would ever use . . . there was no place on earth that had bad reception.

Santa decided to create delivery "teams," with one member of the Clandestines working with three fairy-tale friends. This made up four teams, so Santa divided the world into four sections. As the briefing at the North Pole began and assignments were being made, it was clear that coordinating the distribution of toys from work-shop headquarters to the four regions of the world was going to demand the greatest of organizational skills. He needed the best of the best.

"I need someone with exceptional organizational skills, and I need him fast!" Santa said aloud.

"Oddly enough, Santa, the man for that job is already here, living with all your other elves," Agatha said. She turned to the sea of red-and-green-costumed little people who filled the work-shop. "Hey, Rump, you out there somewhere?"

From the back of the hall came a voice, shouting, "Goldman! How many times do I have to tell you, it's no longer Rump or Stiltskin. It's Goldman!"

From the corner of his eye, Goldman spotted

Imogene and shuddered in shame now that she knew his true identity.

"No one is more qualified for the job, Santa Claus," Agatha explained. "Before Goldman joined the Clandestines, he handled the global distribution of gold for the richest families in the world." Then in a hushed voice she told Santa, "He never really cared about the money. He just liked being part of the families, which was probably why he fit in so well with your family of elves here at the North Pole."

When Goldman saw that Imogene was beginning to smile upon hearing all of this, he started to blush. "Come on, Agatha!" he protested. "Stop talking about me. I'll do whatever you need, Santa. Just stop talking about me!"

"Done!" Santa exclaimed. "Goldman, I'm

naming you chief North Pole dispatcher. There's gonna be a lot of traffic tonight, son. I'll need you to be at the top of your game!"

"Yes, Santa," Goldman said as Imogene gave him a wink. He failed to hide his smile.

Santa's chief tech engineer quickly hooked up the communications system between the four teams and Santa. They could Skype him at any time, and should he need to see what was going on, he could easily link up with the video cameras strapped to their heads.

Before taking off for their various assignments, Santa decided to make time for one Christmas Eve tradition he just couldn't bear to abandon: the pre-flight toasting ceremony where he and his helpers raised a mug of hot cocoa with extra marshmallows and shouted, "Merry Christmas!"

This, as you've probably guessed, was way too sweet for the Clandestines, so each and every one of them spit out the cocoa and took a sip of Barnaby's thistleweed drink instead. Granted, it seemed to sharpen their night vision, which they had to admit was particularly *good* for them that night. But at least it still had a nasty bitter taste, which helped remind them of the *bad* attitudes they all agreed to maintain throughout the night.

CHAPTER 10

The View from Up Here

T HE THING THAT SURPRISED Santa most that Christmas Eve night wasn't the catastrophes. It was that there weren't any. The Drama Queen's Mirror-to-Mirror connections functioned perfectly. They even showed the teams how to blend in and deliver their gifts according to regional traditions. Santa could see what was happening in every location. Goldman's shipping skills proved to be the envy of every overnight delivery system on earth, and his strategically located distribution centers were perfectly accessible to the four delivery teams.

What also surprised Santa was how well the inexperienced teams responded to the challenges they faced in the field, given the enormity of the task and the limited time to accomplish it. It would take several volumes to tell you all the amazing things Santa saw, but here's a recap of some of the highlights from that wintery night of nights.

Medoza did something unexpectedly helpful. Before she headed out for that part of Italy where children awaited the witch La Befana flying on her broomstick to deliver gifts on Epiphany, Medoza distributed jars of her magic sleeping potion to the other fairy-tale characters so they could use them should the children on their routes get too restless.

The Drama Queen, whose perfect Telegram Stan disguise had fooled Santa, was able to repeatedly disguise herself as a child's parent telling them they'd better get to sleep or Santa wouldn't be able to deliver his presents. She fooled them all.

Both Agatha and Medoza would use their artistic gifts to quickly put together costumes and a script so they could impersonate Grandfather Frost and his granddaughter Snow Girl for Russian children. And if that wasn't enough, Agatha knew just how to direct the stacking of presents so that Christmas morning photos would be terrific!

The Giant delighted Santa Claus because he was able to stuff presents down chimneys without standing on the roofs and making too much noise.

In France, Santa's helpers wisely postponed arriving until well after the midnight dinner tradition known as Le Réveillon. *C'est magnifique!*

In Mumbai, where big star-shaped paper lanterns hung everywhere and caroling from village to village was so popular, the Drama Queen placed windup music boxes with the villagers' favorite carols in all of the homes.

Beauty and her prince had a truly inspired idea. They sprayed a delightful evergreen scent into the shoes of children who traditionally got their candy and toys placed inside those stinky things.

Jack did a very generous thing. He left most of his personal stash of magic beans in the countries where the soil was more fertile than the economy.

The teamwork improved as the night wore on. It became almost like a beautifully choreographed ballet, with the music the teams were inspired by coming from the traditions of the various countries, villages, and neighborhoods. There were Latin beats, European folksongs, African rhythms, soaring Russian harmonies, Scandinavian symphonies, and hip-hop grooves.

Watching it all evolve from the central Magic Mirror screen adapted to his sleigh, Santa couldn't help but imagine this saga being commemorated someday as a beautiful ballet! He knew they were making history. But an even bigger surprise was yet to come.

CHAPTER 11

The Spirit of Christmas Is ... Magical!

IN THE WEE HOURS of Christmas morning, the fairy-tale characters found themselves back at Santa's workshop, exhausted from spreading Christmas cheer.

"Boy, are my feet killing me," Agatha said, looking for a place to plop down.

The others agreed as they all found somewhere soft to sit. Santa smiled as he looked at his band of makeshift delivery elves. They had all worked hard and done a great job, and he decided they needed to hear that.

"I'm so grateful for your help. Each one of you. Giant, you did a fine job, especially with all the heavy presents."

The large man blushed. "Aw, gee, thanks, Santa."

"Medoza, your quick thinking and sleeping potion for restless children was extraordinary."

"You really think so?" she said as she sat up a little straighter.

"I know so. And Agatha did some of the finest last-minute gift wrapping ever!"

"Oh, you're just saying that." Agatha blushed.

"No, Agatha, our whole team noticed what

a great job you did," Cinderella added. And she meant it.

"And Goldman," Santa shouted proudly, "you were awesome!"

"Yeah! Three cheers for Rumpelstiltskin!" Imogene called out with all the pride of an honest-to-goodness girlfriend. And for the first time in a long time, Goldman didn't mind hearing his whole name spoken out loud.

The little man smiled. "Well, I couldn't have done it without Imogene and her encouragement, support, insight, beautiful red hair, and—"

"That's enough, Goldman. I get it," Santa said, his cheeks a little more rosy than usual.

Then something magical happened. The Drama Queen stood up and looked at the group. Her face, usually all wrinkled with anger and malice, looked smooth and peaceful. She looked almost . . . pretty. And in an almost pleasant voice, she admitted it was a strange yet not-so-bad feeling doing something so disgustingly good for a change. She hated saying it, but she couldn't lie. She'd kind of had a good time.

"Yeah, me too," the Giant said. "I'm feeling good inside, like the whole night was drenched in Fee-Fi-Fo-Fum sauce. The red kind!"

"What on earth has happened to us, Santa?" Agatha asked. "I don't even feel like revenge would be sweet anymore."

A big smile spread across Santa's face. "It's the magic of giving and helping and sharing that's changing you. You've been touched by the spirit of Christmas," he explained.

"Really? How could anything that sounds so

gross feel this good? Is this a virus of some kind, and if so, how long will it last?" Medoza asked, looking horrified.

Santa Claus started to chuckle because these questions were not ones he'd expected to hear. But he was also smiling because these questions were confirming his belief that there was good in *everyone*; that inside the darkest of oyster shells was where the best pearls were to be found. He then went on to explain the truth about Christmas magic to the Clandestines: to keep those feelings, they must continue doing kind things.

It was then that Medoza protested. She had been rotten for far too long. Doing good deeds could never continue.

The Giant agreed.

"Well, it's the choices that all of us make that

tell our stories, and I suppose you'll have to choose where your next story will lead," Santa said. "But, you know, my dear, we did make a deal. Do you want to give Snow White that poison apple now?"

The Drama Queen was unable to answer. It was like she was temporarily frozen before thawing just enough to say she didn't want to lose the good feelings she'd found this Christmas.

The Giant said he didn't want Jack for supper anymore; he just wanted to have fun with everyone.

Agatha suggested they all forget about revenge and have a party. This brought universal cheering and laughter (the not-so-fiendish kind), and at the Drama Queen's insistence, they joined in singing.

> *It's sweet, sweet, sweet, sweet, sweet*
> *Christmas cheer,*

*We repeat, nothing can beat the joy this
time of year.*

And so the fairy-tale characters joined Santa
and all his elves for a wonderful Christmas party
at the North Pole, singing, dancing, and sharing
the spirit of kindness and giving. During the im-
promptu program, the Drama Queen reprised her
singing-telegram role for those who hadn't seen it.
The Giant and Jack did a tap-dance version of the
Nutcracker. Medoza braided Nora's hair, and they
made a plan to start jogging together.

Prince Andrew performed songs from the
Broadway version of *Beauty and the Beast.* Pinocchio
jumped on Geppetto's knee and they did a surpris-
ingly funny spoof on ventriloquists.

Finally, as everyone was getting sleepy, Santa

closed the party by thanking them all, once again, and saying, "God bless us, every—"

Agatha interrupted him, protesting because that was a line from Dickens and they couldn't end this story by stealing a line from Dickens.

Santa apologized, then said, "Cheerio! But be back soon."

The Drama Queen couldn't believe her ears. "Really?" She told Santa Claus that as much as she loved that show (and did a great version of "As Long As He Needs Me"), Santa couldn't end this story with a line from the musical *Oliver*.

"Okay, okay," Santa said. "Merry Christmas to all, and to all a good night."

The End . . . ?

WELL . . . IS THAT REALLY how the story ends?" asked the Queen a bit sadly. "I guess I'll go let all these good feelings begin to fade slowly away. But I'd rather stay and keep them for a *few* more minutes!"

"Yeah, I would too. What's the rush? Can't we stay a little longer?" the Giant asked.

"Hey, come look outside. Oh! You've got to see

this!" Pinocchio pointed toward the windows. The Clandestines followed the heroes outside the workshop into the dark night just before the dawn.

The stars were shining as brilliantly as ever, but now they twinkled in *colors* like Christmas-tree lights. Red, green, and yellow! Purple and blue! There were sparkles of golden-white twinkles as well. They twinkled in patterns like waves on the ocean, growing faster and brighter and filling the whole sky. And just as the sun was beginning to rise on a canvas of sky that was deep navy blue, the sunbeams shot through all those Christmas-light stars and made them jingle like Santa's sleigh bells.

Then BOOM!

They ignited and sparkled ten thousand times more! It sounded like millions of corn kernels popping, peppered with whistles and screams of delight. They opened and blossomed like heavenly flowers—celestial gardens of light from above. And even the coldest Clandestine heart was warmed by the light show of love that morning. It was hard to believe what was happening. Even Medoza had tears in her eyes. And as all of the embers from the lights began to fall gently down to the earth, they didn't burn out like a fire's embers would. They floated together according to color, with an indescribable, breathtaking glow, then gently landed as delicate spheres in the hands of the *new* heroes.

Medoza's green sphere, like the green of the magical forest she'd come from, reminded her that her talent for style had come from her roots. She knew she would be a great costume designer and help other people find their own personal style.

The Drama Queen's sphere sparkled clear blue,

like an ocean so clear she could see to the bottom. Now that she could see beyond her own reflection, she thought of the actress she wanted to be and how she could use her talents to help others find happiness.

The Giant's was yellow, like freshly baked bread rolls, and the recipe didn't include English bones. He hoped his future held classes at the culinary school. Thinking about all the delicious desserts he could make for his friends made him grin.

Goldman's sphere was red, like Imogene's hair. Perhaps the greatest treasure in the world, he thought, was being in love and having a family.

And Agatha's was purple and mauve, like the dresses her daughters wore before they'd become jealous of sweet Cinderella. She no longer needed to control the world or make anyone seem like they were someone they weren't. Still, she knew she could be a great theater director.

"It's not quite as bad as I thought it would be," said the Queen in regard to the light in her hand.

"No, not at all," Medoza agreed. "I guess in this case we were wrong."

"About lots of things, maybe," the Giant admitted.

"Well, no more than one . . . maybe two things," said Goldman as he looked into Imogene's eyes, and she playfully punched his right arm.

"The old days are over," said Agatha. "And I'm excited to see what comes next."

The Clandestine crew looked at the heroes they now considered friends. All of them had golden lights in their hands.

"This can happen again . . . I mean, more than once!" said the Giant, amazed at the sight.

"Of course it can!" Jack responded. "This is what happens to the heroes of all great stories all the time."

"And for every tale *yet* to be told," said Agatha.

As they all lifted the lights in the palms of their hands, they thought of their magical journeys. Then, placing their "endings" over their hearts, these wonderful gifts in their lives, they looked to the sky as a new day was dawning and let the lights flow into their souls. The most profound gratitude filled every one, and *all* of the heroes, both the old and the new, lived happily ever after . . .

THE END

Epilogue

ONE DAY SNOW WHITE was doing ancestral research and found out she had a great-uncle living on the outskirts of the North Pole. Barnaby White was thrilled to discover he was related to Snow White. He wasn't alone in the world anymore, and, what was more, he was part of a royal line. He finally found courage like he'd never known to go be the hero of his own story.

And as he'd promised himself that he'd only leave the Abominable Snow Café to family, he gave the deed to Snow White on the spot. And off he went to obtain his truest heart's desire, something he had always been too embarrassed to even mention: starting his own line of organically grown superfood health drinks.

Snow White finally shed some light on the place and discovered a most awful mess. But she couldn't be happier cleaning it up, whistling her happiest tunes. Beyond the piano, she discovered a stage and knew the café could be the greatest little dinner theater if someone had a mind to make it happen. She called her favorite Drama Queen and said, "I know you've been looking for a theater where you can focus on the work. Well, how about your own?" She remodeled the café with state-of-the-art equipment.

The Drama Queen was beside herself with glee and immediately hired the most creative team she could. Agatha happily took the reins as artistic director, and Medoza stepped in as costume designer. The Giant was hired as the dining hall's head chef and caterer. Turned out he was a genius in the kitchen.

Among the first of their subscribers was Goldman, who had made a very expensive necklace that was far too extravagant a gift for Imogene when they first met, but it was the perfect donation for a theater company that was just starting out. Goldman presented it to the theater as an investment placed in a trust that would fully finance the theater and any show they wanted to produce for the next fifty years.

• • •

One year passed and the original Clandestines returned to the Abominable Snow Café, now the Copper Mine Club and Dinner Theater, for the world premiere of *A Fairy Tale Christmas*. Goldman had asked to become a "reserve" member of the group because he and Imogene were living their dream of having babies and spending *every minute* of their time raising them.

It was true: the Clandestines no longer had any desire, whatsoever, to do anything evil, dastardly, diabolical, sneaky, underhanded, or dishonorable. Word was spreading that these characters were currently just as good as the heroes of the fairy tales they inhabited.

A Fairy Tale Christmas was conceived from their lives, directed and choreographed by Agatha, and adapted from the novella written by the Drama Queen herself. At Santa's suggestion (and since he was also a major contributor to the dinner theater's renovation, she took his suggestions very seriously), she decided to end her show with a curtain-call reprise of Santa's speech to his elves about seeing so much good in the world:

> *Nobody's perfect in every moment,*
> *Even the people who try*
> *Maybe the greatest good some will do*
> *Is still waiting somewhere inside*
> *Just like the darkest of oyster shells is*
> *   where you're gonna find a pearl*

*Inside everyone, when all's said and
done, there's so much good in the
world!*

The show continues to be performed by the Clandestines Theater Company. Ask anyone who's seen the show and they'll tell you the performances would make the Temptations proud!

Important Note

If you'd like to know what the songs from the musical sound like, you can download the Copper Mine Club and Dinner Theater's original cast recording by going to

www.FairyTaleChristmasMusical.com

Also, Santa insisted that a part of the proceeds from this book, soundtrack, and musical go toward the costs of getting toys into the hands of kids who, this season, thanks to all of you, might actually discover how much they're loved and how much good they have buried somewhere deep inside of them.

About the Authors

Courtesy Russ Dixon

Courtesy Jennifer Davidson

MICHAEL MCLEAN has released more than two dozen albums, has written, produced, and directed award-winning films and television commercials, and has annually presented his landmark Christmas production, *The Forgotten Carols,* based on his book, to sold-out audiences throughout the United States since 1991. He and his wife, Lynne, live in Heber Valley. Visit Michael at michaelmcleanmusic.com and FairyTaleChristmasMusical.com.

SCOTT MCLEAN is an actor, songwriter, and playwright. A graduate of The American Academy of Dramatic Arts (NYC) and The National Theatre Conservatory (Denver), Scott lives, creates, acts, and auditions in New York City.